The Gryphon Press

—a voice for the voiceless—

This book is dedicated, with sincere gratitude,
to each person who rescues, fosters, adopts, and takes responsible care of an animal.

For my daughter, Stephanie Prevost, a wonderful young woman who loves animals,
and who conceived the idea for this story. —*J.P.*

In memory of Jim Haskins (1946–2006),
a friend of animals,
a friend of mine. —*J.P.*

To Consie Powell, I can't thank you enough for your wise observations
and generosity in sharing them—you've really helped me grow as an illustrator.
And to my husband, Paul, for keeping me so well fed and hydrated throughout the project.
Mis saludos a la chef! —*A.H.*

Text design by Amelia Hansen
Text set in Berstrom by BookMobile Design and Publishing Services,
Minneapolis, Minnesota
Printed in Canada by Friesens Corporation

Library of Congress Control Number: 2007936275

ISBN: 978-0-940719-06-4

1 3 5 7 9 10 8 6 4 2

A portion of profits from this book will be
donated to shelters and animal rescue societies.

I am the voice of the voiceless:
Through me, the dumb shall speak;
Till the deaf world's ear be made to hear
The cry of the wordless weak.

—from a poem by Ella Wheeler Wilcox, early 20th-century poet

It's Raining Cats
and cats!

written by
Jeanne Prevost

illustrated by
Amelia Hansen

The Gryphon Press
–a voice for the voiceless–

Jim, Mom, and calico Molly arrived home from the animal hospital. As they unlatched the cat carrier and let sleepy Molly out, gray clouds covered the sun, and rain tumbled down.

"Goodness. It's raining cats and dogs!" Mom burst out.

Jim looked out the window for any cats or dogs that might be plunging down from the sky. He saw only sheets of rain. Then he looked at Molly's belly and saw pink, bare skin and four stiff, black threads like twist ties stitching a cut.

"Mommy, look. Molly's hurt!"

"It's okay, Jim," Mom said. "The vet gave her special medicine so that she wouldn't feel any pain."

"Why did she have to have an operation? She wasn't sick."

"If she hadn't had this special operation, Jim, she'd have litters of kittens every year. She'll soon be back to normal."

"But it would be fun to have kittens!" Jim protested.

The cats-and-dogs rain made a sleepy sort of music.
Mom said, "Let's imagine what would happen if Molly
hadn't had this operation . . ."

"Mom!
Why are there cats in the dressers
and cats downstairs?"

"Molly's had kittens."

"Mom!
Why are there cats on the roof
and cats in my room?"

"Molly and
Molly's kittens
had kittens."

"Mom! Why are there cats in the kitchen
and cats in the cabinets?"

"Molly and Molly's kittens'
kittens had kittens."

"Mom!
There are cats on my bed
and cats on my head!"

"It started with Molly.
She gave birth to Dolly, Holly, Prince, and Pete.

Then Dolly gave birth to

Jon

Tom

Veronica

Monica

and Magic.

Holly gave birth to
Mirror, Major, Lacey, and Dicey.

Prince is the father of Duke,
Jones, Duchess, Jasmine,
Jake, and Daley.

Pete is the father of only
Lady and Princess, but . . .

Lady had three families of five in a year. That's . . .

Addison

Bradley

Charlie

Denver

Frankie

Ernest

Glenda

Harriet

Ivan

Jack

Koala

Nutshell

Lenny

Madison

and Oprah.

Next year, she might have fifteen more.

I wonder how many kittens Princess and Addison will have?

Bradley? Charlie?

In one year? In two years? In three years or more?"

"Mommy, there are cats
on the furniture
and cats on the floor!

Cats in the windows,
and cats on the walls!"

Mom! What will we do?"

"Let's call the vet.
Where's the phone?"

"Hello. Veterinary Clinic."

"Hi. We're having an emergency—too many cats."

"We can help. Your cats each need an operation to stop them from having kittens."

"Ohhh, we should have done this
a while ago! Then we'd have only
Molly," said Mom.

"But Mom, what will we do with the cats we have?"

"Let's find them all homes. Can you make a sign that says ADOPT A CAT?"

"Okay. I'll turn my lemonade stand into an ADOPT A CAT stand."

A girl came up to Jim. Holding her mother's hand, she pointed shyly to the black cat, Denver.

When the girl tried to hold him, he jumped down and scooted away.

"Here is Pocahontas instead. She's more gentle," said Jim.

"Mom, we've been here all day, and we've found homes for only two cats."

"I know, Jim," said Mom. "I called the shelter, but they said it's full. I put an ad in the paper a long time ago, but no one answered it."

"Hey, why don't we take them to school and give them away to my friends?"

Next morning:

"Get in, Roolie. Stop yowling. We aren't even moving yet."

"You've gained weight, Pom-Pom."

"Can we get them all in? There. Finally. Whew!"

"All right. We're off to school
with a carload of cats!"

"Hi, would you
like a free cat?"

"No."

"No."

"No."

"Come on, Sally. Why not?"

"We already have three."

"Why not, Danny?"

"Our dog would chase a cat."

"Why not, Jenna?"

"My mom doesn't want hair on the furniture."

"We can't afford to take care of a cat."

"My brother's allergic to cats."

"My mother won't let me have any pets."

"Awww, what a sweet kitty,"
said the custodian, scooping up Abby.

"You'll keep me company at night,
won't you, girl?"

"You're exactly
what my grandmother
wants for her birthday,"
said a boy, lifting up Lulu.

"Okay. Anyone else?
Only two?"

"Doesn't anyone
here want a cat?"

"Mom, what are we going to do?"

"Let's go back in time to when we had only Molly.
We take her to the veterinarian for an operation . . ."

Jim shook his head, blinked his eyes, and looked down at Molly.

She stretched and pawed playfully at her pink toy mouse, purred, and rubbed against Mom's sock.

"Mom, she's acting like herself again!"

Jim imagined hundreds of cats covering the floor,
creeping under the furniture, and clawing at the windows.
"Oh, Molly, I'm so glad you had the operation.
I'll get the catnip!"

Why Your Cat, Like Molly, Should Be Spayed or Neutered

Reproduction. Female cats who are not spayed can become pregnant up to three times per year. Male cats who are not neutered can be responsible for the birth of a multitude of kittens. Animal shelters are usually very overcrowded and often out of cage space. No one knows exactly how many homeless cats there are in the U.S., but estimates range from 60 to 100 *million*. By ensuring that your cat can't have kittens, you will help diminish the enormous problems of overpopulation and homelessness.

Not Enough Homes. Sometimes, as this story demonstrates, it's impossible to find homes for kittens. Many such kittens, as well as cats, puppies, and dogs, are brought to shelters to be cared for and possibly adopted, or they are abandoned to fend for themselves. Tragically, 3 to 4 million cats and dogs are euthanized in shelters every year. Many of these animals include purebreds and are the unwanted offspring of family pets. Offering to give away kittens to persons you don't know may have a less than desirable outcome for the kitten. All cats and kittens should be spayed or neutered before entering a new home, or they may very well contribute to the problem of overpopulation.

What Is Spaying and Neutering? Neutering applies to male animals and is performed by surgically removing the testicles. Spaying applies to female animals and is performed by surgically removing the uterus and ovaries. A licensed veterinarian performs the operation while the pet is under anesthesia. The animal will usually stay at the veterinarian's office for a few hours following the surgery. Depending upon the procedure, your pet may need stitches removed in a week or two. Female cats should be spayed and male cats neutered by five months of age—before they can produce even one litter.

Your spayed or neutered cat will lose the ability and desire to reproduce, as well as the undesirable behaviors that come with fertility. Here's how your pet will benefit:

Your spayed or neutered cat will:
- be healthier.
- feel more content.
- exhibit a more stable temperament.

Your spayed female will NOT:
- attract unwanted males.
- go into heat, cry nervously, and try to get out to find a mate.
- develop uterine infections or be as likely to develop breast cancer.

Your neutered male will NOT:
- be as likely to spray urine to mark territory.
- be as likely to act aggressively toward other animals.
- need to roam to find a mate.
- develop testicular cancer.

Your spayed or neutered pet will NOT:
- become fat or lazy as a result of these surgeries, unless you overfeed.
- lose his or her natural instincts.
- experience a change in his or her basic personality.

Your city or town will NOT have to:
- spend thousands of dollars feeding and controlling unwanted animals.
- handle overturned, spilled, or ransacked trash containers.
- witness the misery of starving and diseased stray animals.
- spend thousands of dollars euthanizing unwanted animals.

Animal Overpopulation. Spaying and neutering are necessary to reduce animal overpopulation. Our choice as animal lovers is to decide whether to regulate the number of animals in a responsible way or to let the number be determined by disease, lack of food and shelter, untreated injuries, and euthanasia. In addition to spaying or neutering your pet, it's important to keep your cat indoors and provide adequate mental and physical stimulation. You may decide to train your cat to accept a harness and leash or provide a safe outdoor enclosure for him. Always fit your cat with a breakaway collar and identification. You'll then have a better chance of being reunited if he escapes from your home when someone doesn't close the door or there is an emergency.

For more information on the benefits of spaying and neutering your pet, visit the Web sites of the ASPCA, the Humane Society of the United States, or SPAY USA.